Weekly Reader Children's Book Club presents

The Pig Who Saw Everything

Dick Gackenbach

A Clarion Book • *The Seabury Press* • *New York*

This book is a presentation of Weekly
Reader Children's Book Club.
Weekly Reader Children's Book Club
offers book clubs for children from
preschool to young adulthood. All
quality hardcover books are selected
by a distinguished Weekly Reader
Selection Board.

For further information write to:
Weekly Reader Children's Book Club
1250 Fairwood Ave.
Columbus, Ohio 43216

This original tale has been elaborated from a story of the
1870's entitled "I Want to See the World" seen in
Uncle Frank's Animal Stories, published by
Americana Review, Scotia, New York.

The Seabury Press,
815 Second Avenue, New York, N.Y. 10017

Library of Congress Cataloging in Publication Data

Gackenbach, Dick.   The pig who saw everything.
"A Clarion book."
Summary: Pig's daring world-wide adventures never
lead him to suspect that he hasn't left the barn.
[1. Pigs—Fiction] I. Title.
PZ7.G117Pi   [E]   77-12741   ISBN 0-8164-3205-8

For Liz Gordon

Henry, a piglet, lived in a small sty inside a large barn.

He shared the sty with an old and good-natured sow named Esther.

Henry had everything a pig could want.

The barn was always nice and warm in winter and always cool in summer.

The mud in the sty stayed soft and moist.

And everyday, the farm boy brought pails filled to the brim with tasty fish tails, egg shells, sweet potato peels and stale bread.

But still the little pig was not content.

"What more could you want?" asked Esther.

"I want to see the world," Henry told her. "That's what I want."

Her small friend puzzled Esther for she was very happy in the comfort of the sty.

"Mercy me," Esther said, "that's a big dream for such a small head."

"Even so," sighed Henry, "I will not be happy until I've seen everything there is to see."

So while Henry spent his days eating tasty slops and sleeping in the warm mud, he dreamed his big dream of seeing the world.

Each day passed much like the day before, until one fine spring morning. The farm boy came at his usual time.

"Pigs, pigs," he called, banging his pails against the sty door. "Come and get it, pigs!"

Because so many flies lived with Henry and Esther, the farm boy did not wish to stay in the sty too long. He dumped their food in the trough as fast as he could and hurried away.

Esther's large snout sniffed the air.

"Hallelujah," she squealed, "I smell rotten bananas."

But Henry didn't give a hoot about his dinner.

"Look, Esther." His voice trembled with excitement. "The boy forgot to close the door."

Esther's head was already in the trough and her mouth was full of bananas. She didn't see that the careless boy had given Henry the chance to make his dream come true.

Henry stood for a moment, with his heart pounding, trying to make up his mind.

Then he ran through the mud and out the open door.

He didn't stop running until he reached the center of the big barn. There, a great happiness came over Henry. He jumped and danced and sang a song.

"Hey, diddlely dee, I'm happy as can be.
I'm glad I'm free
for now I can see
the beautiful world at last."

Henry made himself dizzy spinning round and round, looking this way and then that way.

"My, the world is a big place," he said. "The sides are very high. And look," he gasped, "there's a large hole at the top and it's full of hay. So that is where hay comes from. From a hole at the top of the world."

Henry was very proud to have made so important a discovery.

When Henry calmed down, he began to feel strange standing there, all alone and in the center of the world.

"Oh, dear," he told himself, "I must take care and not get lost."

So he decided to return to the edge of the world. Then Henry began to explore, walking safely along the side.

The first thing he came to, as he followed the wall, was a gaggle of geese.

When the geese saw Henry, they thrust their heads out through the rails of their pen and made a great noise.

"HONK, HONK," they screamed.

Henry had heard this honking many times over the wall of his sty, but he never knew who or what made such a strange sound.

The geese flapped their wings and caused a great commotion. Henry was so upset by all the noise, he hurried on as fast as he could. But as soon as he was past the geese, he felt proud to have seen such an unusual thing.

Very soon, Henry discovered a
sheepfold. He gazed in wonder at the black
faces and great wooly coats.

"BAA, BAA-A-A!" said the sheep.

Henry had heard a baa before, for that
sound too, had floated over the walls of his sty.

"What does Baa mean?" Henry asked.

But the sheep would not say. They just
stared at Henry.

"BAA-BAA," they repeated.

"Oh well," said Henry, "there is much
I will have to tell Esther when I get home.
Good BAA to you," he said.

Still following close to the wall, Henry came upon another stall. Tied in the stall was a fine, long-horned bull.

"Good heavens," said Henry, "you're bigger than Esther!"

The prize bull was a terrible snob. He lifted his head high so Henry could see the gold medal around his neck. Then, with a great flourish, he swished his long tail and chased away all the flies.

"How very clever," thought Henry wistfully, for his own tail was of no use at all.

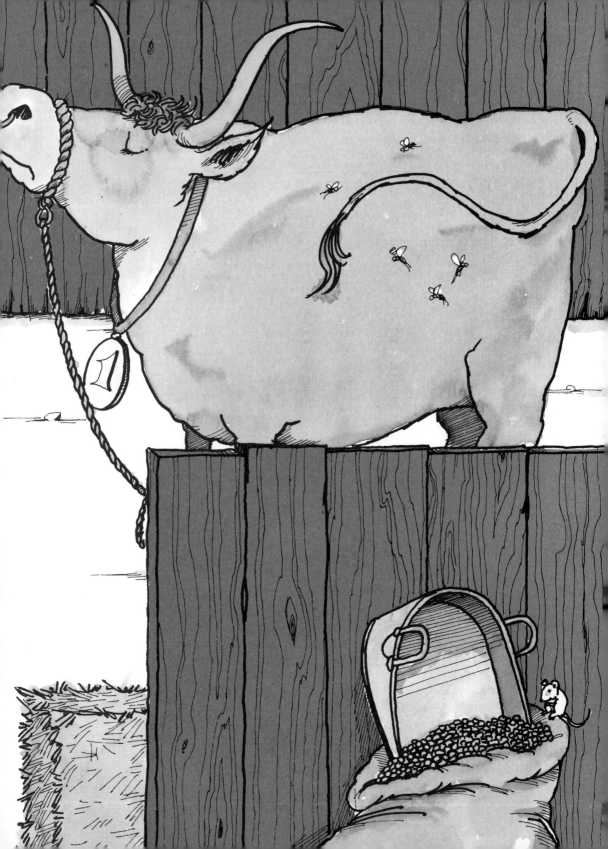

As he continued on his journey, Henry saw cats and chickens, and rats and barn swallows too.

Each new discovery gave Henry a deeper sense of happiness.

"The world is truly a remarkable place," he said.

Finally Henry arrived at a towering door and could go no further.

"This," he decided, "must be the end of the world."

So, thinking he had seen all there was to see, Henry turned and headed for home.

But as soon as the little pig passed the high door, he found himself face to face with the most amazing creature of all.

Henry was shocked by its mighty size. It was twice as big as the great bull.

"What blazing eyes it has," thought Henry. "And such fierce teeth."

Henry was very cautious. He stepped back a few steps and waited to see what the odd creature might do. He was sure it had seen him. The thing remained quite calm and still. Despite its cruel look, it did not seem to mind him being there.

Slowly, Henry moved closer to the beast, careful not to alarm it.

When Henry was as near as he cared to get, he was surprised to discover that the legs of the beast were round and the skin was hard

and shiny. He noticed too, that it made black
and oozy droppings.

"Phew," thought Henry, "I'm glad I
don't share a sty with it."

Henry began to go behind the beast,
hoping to find out what sort of tail it had, when
he was startled by a loud noise.

He looked up and saw the end of the
world open before his very eyes.

A great light poured in through the
opening.

Panic filled the heart of the little pig.
Quickly he turned and fled behind the
nearest stacks of hay. Hiding behind the
hay, Henry watched as a farmer came in
through the great light and approached
the beast.

"Perhaps," thought Henry, "he has
come to feed it."

Instead, and to Henry's amazement, the
farmer touched the shiny skin and the beast
seemed to swallow him whole.

Then, with a horrible roar that sent a chill down Henry's back, the beast ran off through the opening in the side of the world, carrying the farmer inside its belly.

Henry let out a squeal, jumped from his hiding place, and ran back to the sty as fast as he could.

"So," said Esther, "you are home."
She was very happy to see her little
friend again.
"Now tell me," she asked, "what sort of
place is the world?"

"Oh," said Henry, feeling very safe now that he was home again, "the world is both strange and wonderful."

Then he began to tell Esther all about the pigs with wings that go HONK and make a great commotion.

"My goodness," said Esther.

He told Esther
about the pigs
with black faces
and wooly coats.
　　"Did you ever!"
exclaimed Esther.

And about the pig with horns and a long
tail.

"Heaven help us," said Esther.

Then Henry told Esther about the queerest pig of all. The gigantic pig with round legs that ate the farmer.

"There is only one such pig in all the world," Henry said.

"I am thankful for that," sighed Esther. "But was all that worth missing the bananas? They were so good, I ate them all."

"Oh yes, it was worth it," said Henry, triumphantly. "And the very next time the door is left open, we shall both go and see the world together."

"We'll see," said Esther, "we'll see."
Then they both settled down in the warm
mud for a nap.